Oath Keeper

AMY LAURENS

OTHER WORKS

Find other works by the author at
www.amylaurens.com

Oath Keeper

INKLET #38

AMY LAURENS

Inkprint PRESS

www.inkprintpress.com

Print ISBN: 978-1-925825-37-4
eBook ISBN: 9781393193586

www.inkprintpress.com

National Library of Australia Cataloguing-in-Publication Data
Laurens, Amy 1985 –
Oath Keeper
32 p.
ISBN: 978-1-925825-37-4
Inkprint Press, Canberra, Australia
1. Fiction—Fantasy—Dragons & Mythical Creatures 2. Fiction—Fantasy—Military 3. Fiction—Short Stories

First Print Edition: July 2020
Cover image © Mark Frost via Pixabay
Cover design © Inkprint Press
Interior art © Amy Laurens

OATH KEEPER

THE METALLIC SCENT OF BLOOD reached him through the sharpness of the snow. For a moment, his heart leapt and he thought the battle was still raging, the cries of dying men filling his ears and stopping his senses; but no. The mountains up ahead were the foothills of home, and there were no people around, no sounds, no battle cries.

Easing his shoulders under heavy mail—he hadn't dared leave it behind, old Tom would curse him halfway to the grave if he returned without it—he trudged on.

The path crested and he spotted the source of the blood-scent easily: a great dragon, rear half skinned, muscle and sinew left exposed to the elements. Blood had seeped into the snow around it, tinting it pink.

He ran a hand over his face. He'd been at battle for nine and a half months. The war was supposed be over. Coming home was supposed to be the end of all the carnage.

But no, someone had to drop a stinking great dead dragon in his path. He gritted his teeth, hefted his pack, and trudged towards the beast.

Halfway there the bushes off the side of the path rustled. He barely had time to check that his sword was still in its scabbard before five scruffy-looking bandits appeared, three bearing equally scruffy swords covered in nicks and dings. The other two held rough-hewn bats, and one tried for menacing as he tapped his bat against his free palm.

The soldier sighed and eased his sword free. He could take the five of them with his eyes closed—but probably not if he tried to keep them all alive. Gods, he was so *tired* of death.

The leader of the bandits swaggered forward. "Come t' steal our dragon, have ye?"

"Put your sword down, mate. All I want to do is go home." The soldier shifted his grip on his own sword in case the bandit lunged.

In response, the bandit sneered. "That's what they all say." He turned to his lackeys. "All right, boys. You know what to do."

He gave them the nod and as one they advanced towards the soldier.

"Please," he said, holding his sword up loosely in one hand. "I won't fight you. I won't fight any longer. Somewhere the fighting must stop. Please, let it be here, now."

The bandits laughed.

"Easy pickings, this one," one of the men said.

"Surprised he came back from the war alive," mused another.

The soldier bowed his head. "So be it," he said. "I vowed not to take a life outside of war, and I will not break that now."

He held the sword out in front of him, one hand balancing the grip, the other lightly cupping the flat of the blade.

Gods preserve us all.

Magic crackled around him. *You do well, oath-keeper. You are worthy.*

A creaky rumble sounded, and before anyone could react, the great dragon's tail swept right through the midst of the bandits, knocking them all off their feet.

Three were immediately rendered unconscious, and without hesitation the solider leapt forward to follow up on his advantage, knocking out a fourth with the flat of his blade.

If the only way to avoid death today was to leave them sleeping on the ground, well, his oaths had prohibited murder, not violence.

The soldier pivoted as the leader of the bandits cried out and lunged at his shoulder, but the soldier ducked and let the stroke go past.

He dodged left, dropped to one knee and drove upwards with the pommel of his sword, aiming for the bandit leader's chin. A nice, steady uppercut ought to do it.

The dragon's claws caught him around the leg, destabilised him.

His arms windmilled.

The sword twisted point up. The bandit completed his lunge, the sword driving deep into his throat.

Arterial blood spurted, red and bright, life gushing from the man before his eyes.

War cries sounded in the soldier's ears, the smell of blood blocked out thought, and the pounding of a thousand warrior feet shook the ground. *No. No, I promised!*

The soldier barely felt it as the dragon shifted its grip and dragged him closer. The smell of rotting meat on the great carnivore's breath mingled with blood until it could have belonged to week-old bodies decaying on the fields, and the pain that lanced through him as the dragon bit down was the piercing of swords. He stared glassy-eyed at the sky as death descended.

A moment passed in rippling pain, and the soldier realised he was on his feet, facing the great dragon while blood dribbled from his shoulder. He clamped down on the wound, noted that the dragon's skin now covered nearly three-quarters of its body, and gazed up at the great iridescent eye.

The dragon turned its head, staring pointedly to where the bandit leader lay dead in a pool of his own blood.

Guilt stung the soldier's chest; he gulped down air like a man drowning.

Gently, the dragon nudged him with a nose whose nostrils wafted smoke, and the soldier fell down beside the bandit.

"What?" he shouted. "What do you want from me? If you'd just stayed out of it I could have knocked him out! You, you made me kill him. This is your fault!"

But the dragon simply stared at him, waiting.

Tears streaming down his cheeks, the soldier gathered up the bandit in his arms. Yes, the bandit had initiated the attack, and yes, it couldn't be doubted that the corpse in front of him had belonged to a bad man. But his vows. To lose them over such a sense-less death.

He'd had enough of senselessness. He pressed his forehead to the bandit's. "I'm sorry," he whispered. "I didn't mean for you to die."

The bandit stirred in his lap, head tossing, eyes twitched beneath closed lids. The wound in his neck ceased bleeding; the skin began infinitesimally to seal.

The soldier's gaze flicked to his own shoulder, where the bite mark had nearly closed beneath the tear in his chain-mailed shirt, then to the dragon, who was now fully clothed in skin again but for its tail.

You would have sacrificed yourself to preserve your oath. Now you may keep it forever. The dragon stretched like a cat waking from a nap, extended its wings with a single mighty flap, and leapt into the sky.

"Thank you," the soldier mur-
mured, eyes wide. "Thank you."

THE MAKING OF
OATH KEEPER

I was practising flash fiction, I'm pretty sure. It was probably for the same course that brought us both the stories in Inklet #30 (*Anything For You* and *As Long As I Live*).

I remember imagining a soldier, coming home from a war he hadn't wanted to fight in the first place, and wondering: what does this man want more than anything else in the world?

Peace, I decided. It seems to me that no one longs for peace so much as those who've had to dwell in its opposite for any length of time.

And, for someone who hadn't wanted to fight in the first place, to never need kill anyone again.

The story spiralled out from there.

DOWNLOAD YOUR FREE EBOOK

When you buy a print book from Inkprint Press, we like to say THANK YOU by offering you the ebook for free!

Please head to www.inkprintpress.com/inklets/38/ and the use the coupon 38INK to get your copy of this Inklet in epub AND mobi today!
(Coupon will only work once.)

Read more by Amy Laurens!

DREAMING OF FORESTS

There was a forest. That was the simple fact of the matter: there was a forest now, and there hadn't been before. Deena let the tent flap drop closed in front of her, inhaled steadily, and tried again.

Nope, still forest. She bit her lip, debating: go out and explore, or hide in the tent?

In the end, exploration won for the simple, practical reason that nature, as it were, was calling. So she caterpillared her way out of her downy sleeping bag, pulled her hiking shorts on over the black, fleecy leggings she'd slept in, zipped up her polar fleece jumper, crammed her grandmother's knitted beanie over her brown hair, and pushed her way outside.

The other tent was gone. For a moment, that made her pulse race—

but then the reality of her sur-
roundings overtook her senses. The air
inside the tent had been warm, musty.
The air outside yester-day had smelled
of the sea, a salty tang with just a hint
of rotting seaweed.

Today, the air smelled like sap, and
living things, a green smell she asso-
ciated with her grandmother's garden
thanks to that summer she'd spent
there when she was twelve, when
they'd spent hours of days of weeks
pruning and twining and tending, re-
turning to the house only for meals
and sleep, hands crusty with black dirt
her grandmother called gold, under-
nails caked with the stuff, elbows and
knees stained black—and green.

This, Deena thought, was what
every green scratch-and-sniff thing
should smell like. Forget your apple,
forget your lime; *this* was green. She
inhaled deeply, and despite the oddity
of the situation, felt her eyes light up

as her body relaxed, melting into the space while at the same time inflated, buoyed, full. Something about this wondrous, spontaneous forest was familiar—and right.

She had no idea what the trees were, but they were tall, straight as ship masts or indigenous spears, thick and thin, rough-barked but paler than stringy barks, a brownish-grey, and the tiny, emerald, coin-sized leaves looked soft as butter, soft as petals.

Deena had tried keeping plants in their third-floor apartment back home, but somehow she could never remember to water them enough, or else she watered them too much and they died, thin and pustulant. She cried, every time, as her mother shook her head and made Deena walk them down to the communal skip bins in the alleyway behind the complex.

Her grandmother had consoled her on the phone each time, had promised that one day she'd have plants aplenty, more than she knew what to do with.

But one day wasn't soon enough for Deena—which was why she'd taken up hiking, of course. If she couldn't have plants at home, by golly was she going to surround herself with them in her spare time. So a forest? Amazing.

The other tent, her friends, vanishing? Less so.

Nature was still calling.

And the current cover situation was a little thin for her liking; yesterday, there'd been a handy thicket of salt bushes and something vaguely acacia-like between the grass and the sand dunes. Today, it was just open forest all the way down to the sand behind and to her right, and all the way up to the mountains ahead and to the left.

On the other hand, there didn't seem to be anyone else around.

Sighing, she attended to her body's needs, butt cheeks momentarily icing over as a wind whipped down from the mountain, setting the trees rushling and shushling—but it seemed like a freak gust and nothing more, and soon enough she was clothed and warm again—and hungry.

A brief forage in the tent revealed a couple of muesli bars tucked into the pocket of her raincoat, and of course, there were the packet soups in her hiking pack, and she still had a couple of litres of water. Nothing to heat it with, though; Rachel had had the Trangia in her pack, and some time in the night— as was pretty usual, these days—she'd snuck into the boys' tent, taking her pack with her for a pillow. Which meant that all of the above—Rachel, boys, tent, packs, and cooking stove— were now gone.

Deena sat heavily on the stump by the front of the tent and dropped her chin into her hands.

It wasn't that she'd never believed

in magic before—she'd seen her grandmother's garden, after all, and although she'd stopped protesting to the contrary so people would stop protesting her sanity, she knew full well she'd seen creatures in her grandmother's garden when she'd been little that had no right existing on this mortal plane.

But on the other hand, until now, magic had been content to merely linger in the background, a blurred, bokehed backdrop to real life, something vaguely sensed, but never fully realised.

What, Deena wondered, had made the difference today? Why now suddenly jump arrestingly into the foreground?

Or, she wondered, gazing around as the trees whispered secretively, why *here*?

Hmm. That seemed like a crucial question.

The tent, she felt, was light enough. It would be a bit of a headache to get the whole thing into her pack with her camping mat—yesterday, Rachel had been carrying half the tent, but that clearly wasn't an option today, and neither was leaving the tent behind— but she should be able to manage. Because as she saw it, she could either sit here all day, hoping and wondering whether the others would come back—or she could go explore this magical, magical forest that even now was layering calm over her like blankets, like she belonged here, and *find out* what had happened to the others.

It took about thirty minutes, moving purpose-fully, to down a couple of muesli bars, swirl a packet of soup into one of the water bottles and gag it down, and pack up all the gear. It did fit in her pack—only just, and she'd had to let all the straps out, but it wasn't too heavy, just bulky.

And so, with the legs zipped onto her hiking shorts, turning them into pants once more, with her heavy boots on and her beanie still crammed over her hair and her hands deep in the pockets of her emerald-green polar fleece jumper, and her dark blue pack sticking up over her head and weighing down her hips, Deena set off through the trees that had miraculously appeared, heading back approximately the way they'd come in the evening before.

Keep reading! Head to
www.amylaurens.com/books/novellas/dreaming-of-forests/
to buy your copy now!

ABOUT THE AUTHOR

AMY LAURENS is an Australian author of fantasy fiction for all ages. She has written the award-winning portal-fantasy *Sanctuary* series about Edge, a 13-year-old girl forced to move to a small country town because of witness protection (the first book is *Where Shadows Rise*), the humorous fantasy *Kaditeos* series, following newly-graduated Evil Overlord Mercury as she attempts to acquire a castle, the young adult *Storm Foxes* series about love and magic and mental health, and a whole host of non-fiction.

INKLET #031
Welcome to Dark Dale
LIANA BROOKS

INKLET #032
When War Came to Town
A Powers Story
AMY LAURENS

INKLET #033
Not Fantasy
AMY LAURENS

INKLET #034
Courting the Winter Prince
LIANA BROOKS

INKLET #035
At the Home of the Winter King
A Storm Foxes Story
AMY LAURENS

INKLET #036
With This Ring
AMY LAURENS

DOUBLE ISSUE
INKLET #037
Venus &
Seven Reasons I Said No
LIANA BROOKS

INKLET #038
OATH KEEPER
AMY LAURENS

INKLET #039
FORGET
A Powers Story
AMY LAURENS

NOT QUITE
Cinderella
LIANA BROOKS
ONE BAD MAN
AMY LAURENS
DOUBLE ISSUE
The Claustrophobia
Of Loneliness &
Adam, Be A Star
AMY LAURENS
The Artist
as a Young Girl
LIANA BROOKS
CONFESSIONS
AMY LAURENS
But For Snow
A Kaieous Story
AMY LAURENS
The Boy
Named NO
LIANA BROOKS
Anamata
AMY LAURENS
A Wolf FOR
Christmas
AMY LAURENS